By Trey King
Illustrated by Kenny Kiernan

SCHOLASTIC INC.

ISBN 978-0-545-82555-9

10 9 8 7 6 5 4 16 17 18 19 20/0

Printed in the U.S.A. 40

First printing 2015

Designed by Angela Jun

There's a fire in LEGO® City! The firefighters are on their way to help.

Ricky is a firefighter in training. He will spend one year learning the ropes!

60002

A Dumpster is on fire!

First, the firefighters make sure no one is in danger. Then, they get ready to fight the fire.

That fire doesn't stand a chance against me!

But Ricky doesn't wait. He grabs the hose and tries to put out the fire on his own.

The hose is too strong for one person! Water sprays everywhere.
Whoaaaaa!

"Ricky, you've got a lot to learn," Chief Rita says. "You need to work with the team. I will help train you, but you have to listen. By next summer, you will be a *great* firefighter."

A few months later, it is fall.
Ricky is taking a nap . . .
Zzzzzzzzz
RIIIIIING!!
. . . until the fire alarm goes off!
Then he swings down the pole.

"A firefighter must always be ready!" says Rita. "Don't forget your helmet!"

There was an accident at the race course. Luckily, no one was hurt. But the rider landed in a tree. It's up to the firefighters to rescue him.
Good thing this tree caught me!
Meow!

While the other firefighters put out the fire, Rita and Ricky help the rider.

"Awww," Ricky says. "I wanted to put out the fire!"

"Putting out fires is important," Rita explains, "but it's *more* important to make sure people are safe."

Winter comes early and brings lots of snow. The sidewalk is very slippery.

Ricky wants to build a snowman outside. But Rita calls him in to work.

"We need to shovel and put out salt on the sidewalk so no one falls," Rita explains. "Thinking ahead is what good firefighters do. That means stopping bad things before they happen."

You can't put out a fire with a shovel!

The next day, the alarm goes off.

The firefighters race outside to the truck. The sidewalk has no ice or snow. “Good thing we shoveled and salted,” says Ricky.

RIIIIIING!!

It is spring, and the fire department is busy! A call comes in. This time, Ricky is ready. He is prepared with all the tools a firefighter needs—including his lunch!

I'm ready! But where is everybody?

Rita and Ricky fly a helicopter to the fire.
Ricky can see all of LEGO City from up there!

A powerboat's engine got too hot and caught fire. But the firefighters get to the scene fast to help.

Rita flies the helicopter while Ricky saves the boat driver.

FIRE 60002

Soon, the rest of their team arrives to help, too.
Together, the firefighters put out the fire on the boat.
FIRE 60002

"How did I do, Chief?" Ricky asks.
"You did great," Rita says.
Nothing beats being rescued—except pizza!

60002

By summertime, things are really heating up. A big fire breaks out. The entire fire department rushes to save the day.

Two buildings are on fire! Both are old and empty, but the firefighters need to put out the fire quickly.

First, Ricky makes sure all of the people in the area are safe.

Let's move over this way, folks.

Thinking ahead, Ricky helps hook up the fire truck to the fire hydrant. Now, he and his team are ready to fight the fire.

Finally, Ricky calls out to the rest of his team to help him put out the large fire. It takes several men and women to hold a fire hose steady.
On the count of three! One . . . two . . .

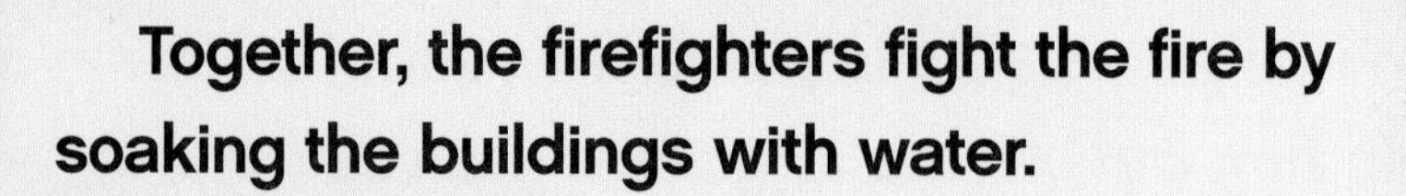

Together, the firefighters fight the fire by soaking the buildings with water.

OOSH!

Soon, the fire is out, and the city is safe.

Ricky thinks it is exciting to help put out the fire with his team.

"It looks like our work here is done," Ricky tells Rita.

"And it looks like your rookie days are over," Rita says. "Good job!"

SMACK!

FIRE 60002

"You've worked so hard all year, and now you're a firefighter," Rita says. "What are you going to do now?"

"Take a day off!" Ricky says.